W9-CLJ-710

Ultra-Violet Catastrophe!

Ultra-Violet Catastrophe!

or The Unexpected Walk with Great-Uncle Magnus Pringle

story *by* MARGARET MAHY

pictures *by* BRIAN FROUD

PARENTS' MAGAZINE PRESS/NEW YORK

Text copyright © 1975 by Margaret Mahy
Illustrations copyright © 1975 by J. M. Dent & Sons Ltd., London
All rights reserved. Library of Congress catalog card number: 74-12445
Printed in the United States of America
A Pippin Paperback published by Parents' Magazine Press
10 9 8 7 6 5 4 3 2 1

Ultra-Violet Catastrophe! is published in a hardcover edition by
Parents' Magazine Press, 52 Vanderbilt Avenue, New York, N.Y. 10017
ISBN 0-8193-0908-7

Ultra-Violet Catastrophe!

Sally's mother stood underneath a big tree looking up into its branches.

"Sally!" she called. "Are you there?"

"She isn't here," Sally called back. "Something has eaten her. It's dangerous up here."

"Sally, come down at once!" her mother called again.

Sally shut her eyes and answered, "I'm not Sally. I'm Horrible Stumper the tree pirate."

But it was no use. Horrible Stumper the tree pirate had to come down out of the leaves and the smell of spring and turn into Sally once more.

Sally shut her eyes...

Sally was washed around the face and scrubbed around the knees. She had to put on her best dress and her long white socks. Her hair was brushed until it shone and her ears went all red and hot. She was being taken to visit her mother's cousin, Aunt Anne Pringle.

Aunt Anne lived in the country, but not on a farm. Her house was called "Sunny Nook," and it was full of things Sally was not allowed to touch.

"She doesn't like me even to *breathe*," Sally said crossly. "She fusses and fusses all the time."

"You'll have to manage somehow," replied her mother. "I know Aunt Anne is fussy, and I know there are no children to play with, but you can't expect everything to suit you all the time...Oh dear, your knees still look dirty."

"It's the scratches," Sally explained. "I could paint faces on my knees and then the scratches wouldn't show."

"Come on!" said Sally's mother in rather a sharp voice. "Hurry up, or we'll be late."

They caught the bus in time.

Sally had hoped that they would miss it.

"Oh dear, your knees still look dirty."

unt Anne met them at the door of Sunny Nook. Sally could tell at once that she had not improved. She was tiny, and terribly clean and neat. She looked more like a freshly dusted china ornament than any real person. She smiled at Sally, and then talked over her head to her mother.

"I have Father staying with me for a month," she said. "It's rather awkward. Old men can be so difficult, and he's very set in his ways, you know. The things he says! Sometimes I don't understand just what he's getting at, he uses such funny long words."

Sally's mother made an "I'm-sorry-to-hear-that" clicking sound with her tongue.

They went into Aunt Anne's tiny sitting-room.

Aunt Anne met them at the door of Sunny Nook.

There on the flowery couch was a very clean, scrubbed-and-scoured, washed-up and brushed-down little old man.

Sally thought Aunt Anne must have rinsed him out, then starched and ironed him, and *then* polished him with a soft cloth.

"This is Sally, Father," said Aunt Anne. "I told you a dear little girl was coming to visit."

Sally's mother thought she saw a Horrible Stumper look coming onto Sally's face. She began to talk quickly. "Sally, this is Great-Uncle Magnus Pringle."

Great-Uncle Magnus looked at Sally from under his wrinkly eyelids.

"Ultra-Violet Catastrophe to you, young lady," he said mysteriously. His voice was loud—loud but not crackly. It was rather like guns at sea.

"Oh, don't start talking that rubbish!" said Aunt Anne fretfully. "Look, why don't you two take each other for a walk?"

Mother and Aunt Anne led Sally and Great-Uncle Magnus out of the house and pointed them down the road towards the corner.

"Be good and keep clean," said Aunt Anne.

Great-Uncle Magnus looked at Sally…

Sally and Great-Uncle Magnus walked along the country road in the country sunshine smelling the country smells of wet grass and cows.

They came to a thick dark hedge speckled with little white flowers.

Suddenly Great-Uncle Magnus stopped.

"Do you like to go through hedges?" he asked. "*I* do, and it's years since I've been through a good hedge."

Sally stared at Great-Uncle Magnus, amazed at such thoughts in a great-uncle.

"I see a hole in this hedge," went on Great-Uncle Magnus, "and I'm going through it...it would be a help to have you give me a hand on the other side."

"Shall I go first then?" asked Sally. "In case of danger?"

"That would be kind of you," said Great-Uncle Magnus. "I have this creaky knee, you see. It's a good knee, mind you. I've had it for years, but it *is* creaky."

Sally scrambled through the hole in the

"I see a hole in this hedge..."

hedge, smelling its special hedge smell as she went. The hedge tried to hold onto her, as hedges do, but she got through safely. After her came Great-Uncle Magnus, breathing hard.

"Ah," he said, as Sally helped him up, "that was good. That was refreshing. Now what have we here?"

On the other side of the hedge the ground was swampy from yesterday's rain. In between the grass, muddy water was oozing. Grass tufts stuck out of puddles.

"It's a long time since I went wading," said Great-Uncle Magnus thoughtfully.

"What are you doing?" cried Sally.

"Taking my shoes and socks off," the great-uncle replied, and so he was.

Sally grinned. She sat down beside Great-Uncle Magnus and took off her shoes and her long white socks, too. She had to help the great-uncle with a tightly tied shoelace.

"Your Aunt Anne always ties my shoelaces as if she were choking the shoes to death," said Great-Uncle Magnus.

"Taking my shoes and socks off..."

Great-Uncle Magnus's pale feet sank greedily into the mud.

"Ah!" he sighed, "there's something about mud, eh? Nothing else has quite that—that—that *muddy* feel, has it?"

Sally was amazed again. She had not expected to find a great-uncle who felt the same way about mud as she did.

"Ultra-Violet Catastrophe," murmured the great-uncle to himself.

"What does that mean?" asked Sally boldly.

"It's the *sound* I say it for, not the meaning," Great-Uncle Magnus explained. "Some people say 'Goodness Gracious.' That doesn't mean much—they say it for the sound. But *I* like to say something that sounds even better and more important."

"Words usually mean some real thing," said Sally carefully. "For instance, I say 'Horrible Stumper' and it means a tree pirate. Don't your good-sounding words mean anything?"

"They *do* mean something scientific," admitted Great-Uncle Magnus. "Something scientific and too hard to explain." He started

"Ultra-Violet Catastrophe," murmured the great-uncle.

to splash his way through the grass and mud. He had a muddy patch on the back of his trousers where he had been sitting down.

"You see," he said, as he went along, "Annie's a good girl and she means well—but she treats me like one of her potted plants. She waters me and puts me in the sun and leaves me alone. Serve her right if I grew up the wall and put out flowers! After a while I begin to think I'm really turning into a potted plant, and then I sing to myself or use long words—'Ultra-Violet Catastrophe,' I say, or 'Seismological Singularity.'"

"That's a *hard* one," said Sally with great respect.

"Too hard for a potted plant!" Great-Uncle Magnus nodded. "No mere potted plant would use words like that. *Then* I know that I'm Magnus Pringle all the time."

They came down to a clear stream flowing over brown stones. On the bank above the stream a green tree spread wide rough arms. Great-Uncle Magnus's sharp old eyes looked up into the green arch above them.

"You see," he said, as he went along...

"It's years since I climbed a tree, years and years," said Great-Uncle Magnus. "I'd climb this one if it wasn't for my fear of the tree pirates."

"Oh, well—I'll just go up and check for you," Sally offered eagerly. "This is too good a tree to waste! And once I'm up, I can help you if your knee creaks, or if it's too hard for you or anything."

"There's nothing like a tree," Great-Uncle Magnus remarked a few minutes later, still down below. "It's good to look up in the air with the leaves all around. What do *you* think?"

"'Ultra-Violet Catastrophe,' *I* think," answered Sally boldly.

"Just what I was thinking myself," said Great-Uncle Magnus. "Seismological Singularity! I think I'll sing a bit."

He pointed his nose to the sky and began:

> *"Boiled beef and carrots,*
> *Boiled beef and carrots."*

Sally felt very happy, sitting up there in the tree listening to Great-Uncle Magnus.

He pointed his nose to the sky and began to sing.

Everything felt very alive ... the tree with its branches and bark and its spring leaves bright against the blue sky. Sally pointed her nose at the sky, too, and felt the sun shine through the leaves in hot spring freckles on her face. The tree at home and the tree here were like sunny rooms in open rustling houses. She looked down at the stream below.

"Is it years and years since you made a dam across a creek?" asked Sally.

"How did you guess?" Great-Uncle Magnus said wonderingly. "It was certainly a long time ago. I see some good stones down there, too."

Somehow, neither Sally nor Great-Uncle Magnus were as tidy as they had been when they set out.

Making a dam did not improve things. When you are making a dam it is easy to get damp and muddy around the edges. They built a good dam out of mossy green and brown stones. But the cunning water found a way over, or around, or through, and kept them busy and silent for quite a long time.

They built a good dam.

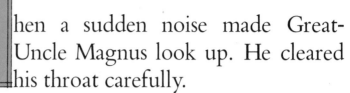hen a sudden noise made Great-Uncle Magnus look up. He cleared his throat carefully.

"Sally," he said, "don't be frightened, but just look behind you and tell me what you see."

Sally looked under her arm at the bank behind her. A large brown-and-white cow was standing there, watching them. She had a very young brown-and-white calf beside her. She had very sharp horns. As Sally looked, she put her head down and pointed her horns at them. She gave a grumbling, angry "Moo!"

"Having a new calf can make a cow very cross," Great-Uncle Magnus said, gathering up his socks and shoes. "Not that I'm frightened of a mere cow, but still...."

"A cow with a calf isn't as mere as other cows, I don't think," said Sally, gathering her socks and shoes, too.

The cow started to come down the bank at them. Sally and Great-Uncle Magnus moved quickly. Sally was amazed at the speed a great-uncle can put on when there is an angry cow coming down a bank after him.

Sally was amazed at the speed a great-uncle can put on.

There was no hedge on the other side of the creek, but there was a barbed-wire fence. Socks and shoes were tossed across. Then Sally scrambled over it. As she did so, she heard the hem of her dress tear open. A moment later Great-Uncle Magnus's trousers ripped, too.

Sally and Great-Uncle Magnus stood staring at each other, while the cow mooed angrily at them from the other side of the fence. Then her calf called, and she hurried back to it. And, at that very moment, like other anxious, mooing cows, Sally's mother and Aunt Anne came calling down the road.

Great-Uncle Magnus shook his head slowly. "I can't see myself," he said, "but I don't think your mother is going to be pleased with *your* appearance."

"I don't think Aunt Anne will be pleased with yours, either," Sally told him. They were both wet and muddy and stained and torn.

There was a barbed-wire fence...

There was a most terrible fuss!

"How *could* you, Father, how *could* you!" Aunt Anne cried.

"It just happened, Annie," said Great-Uncle Magnus in a humble voice.

Aunt Anne made them stand on newspapers in the path, while she brushed them and cleaned them as much as she could.

"It's just as well you're going home at the end of the week," she said to Great-Uncle Magnus. "I couldn't stand another adventure like this!"

"Very sorry, Annie," said Great-Uncle Magnus, still more humbly. Then he looked at Sally's mother. "Why don't you and Sally come to visit me when I go home?" he asked. "I've got a little place by the shore, and a little boat I putter about in. I catch a few fish from the end of the wharf. You wouldn't be bored."

Aunt Anne made them stand on newspapers...

"We'd love to come," said Sally's mother. (She wasn't as upset as Aunt Anne, being used to mud and torn skirts.) "I can see you two get on well together," she added.

"We've got a lot in common," Great-Uncle Magnus agreed.

They had been so long on their walk, there was scarcely time for Sally to have a bite to eat before getting ready to go home.

Sally and Great-Uncle Magnus looked at each other and could not find the right words to say goodbye, even though it was only for a short time.

"Hurry, Sally, we'll miss the bus," called her mother.

Sally suddenly knew the exact thing to say. "Ultra-Violet Catastrophe!" she shouted back, as her mother waved to Aunt Anne with one hand and tugged her with the other.

Great-Uncle Magnus brightened up. "Horrible Stumper to *you*, young lady!" he replied. "I couldn't ever hope to go on a country walk with a better tree pirate than you."

Great-Uncle Magnus brightened up…

Margaret Mahy grew up in a little town "where the river met the sea, close under the hills covered with dense New Zealand bush." When she was very young, Ms. Mahy wrote stories for her school magazine and for the children's page of a local newspaper. She had a brief career in nursing, then returned to college and library work. Today she is a librarian and continues to write her fanciful stories for children in a "lovely new house by the sea" where she lives with her two daughters. She has twice won the New Zealand Library Association's Esther Glen Award, and many of her tales have been published in the United States, including a previous book for Parents' Magazine Press, *The Witch in the Cherry Tree.*

Brian Froud was born in Winchester, England, and is a graduate of the Maidstone College of Art. In addition to a growing number of tales for children, he has illustrated book jackets in the realm of adult fantasy as well. Mr. Froud's plans for the future include "building 30-foot models of castles and peopling a wood with models of dwarfs and gnomes." The artist lives in London. *Ultra-Violet Catastrophe!* is his first book for Parents' Magazine Press.